ADRIAN RAESIDE

THE RAINBOW BRIDGE

A Visit to Pet Paradise

Harbour Publishing

Text and artwork copyright © 2012 Adrian Raeside

6 7 8 9 — 21 20 19 18

Harbour Publishing Co. Ltd.
P.O. Box 219, Madeira Park, BC, V0N 2H0
www.harbourpublishing.com

Cover and text design — Anna Comfort O'Keeffe
This book was printed with soy-based inks on chlorine-free paper made with 10% post-consumer waste.
Printed and bound in Canada

BRITISH COLUMBIA ARTS COUNCIL
We acknowledge the support of the Province of British Columbia through the British Columbia Arts Council

Canada Council for the Arts   Conseil des Arts du Canada

Harbour Publishing acknowledges financial support from the Government of Canada through the Canada Book Fund and the Canada Council for the Arts, and from the Province of British Columbia through the BC Arts Council and the Book Publishing Tax Credit.

Library and Archives Canada Cataloguing in Publication

Raeside, Adrian, 1957-

The rainbow bridge / Adrian Raeside.

ISBN 978-1-55017-584-4

I. Title.

PS8585.A298R35 2012   jC813'.54   C2012-900574-6

For Koko and Sakura

For more about the author please visit
www.raesidecartoon.com

It was the perfect summer for a boy and his dog.

Especially for a seven-year-old boy named Rick and his beloved dog, Koko.

The days were long, the weather was hot, and Rick and Koko spent most of their days splashing about in the swimming hole at Bear Creek. Rick would dive under the water, leaving Koko to paddle around, pretending to look for him. Rick would surface and spit water at Koko, then Koko would bark and flick water at Rick with his tail.

After they tired of the water, they'd chase each other through the fields back to the house.

Rick would grab a snack and watch cartoons, while Koko would play with his well-chewed squeaky bone.

It felt like summer would never end and Rick and Koko would play forever.

But like the seasons, all things must change.

As the leaves turned from green to gold and the days got cooler and shorter, Koko seemed to slow down. He didn't run as fast as the wind anymore, he didn't wake Rick up every morning with his wet tongue and blast of bad doggie breath and he lost interest in chasing squirrels up trees. Even his beloved squeaky bone sat un-chewed in the corner of his stinky basket.

Mom thought she knew the reason. "Koko is getting old and needs more rest. Besides, he's fifteen years old. That's a hundred and five in dog years. Much older than you, Ricky!"

Then one frosty December morning, Koko didn't even get out of his basket to see Rick off to school. He lay in his stinky basket, his big brown eyes following Rick around the room as he collected his books and lunch. Rick stroked Koko's head. "Do you think Koko is sick?"

Mom bent down to look at Koko, who whimpered and managed a feeble tail-wag. "I don't know Ricky, but Dad and I will take Koko to the vet this morning."

Rick put Koko in a headlock, scratched him behind his ears and raced out to catch the school bus.

"See you this afternoon, Koko. Don't growl at the doctor," he shouted as he ran out the door.

Rick could barely concentrate on his school work all day, thinking about Koko. He raced home from the school bus, anxious to hear what the vet had said.

Bursting into the kitchen, Rick froze in his tracks. The stinky basket was empty! He looked around the kitchen in a panic. "Where's Koko!?" he shouted.

Mom and Dad were sitting at the kitchen table. It looked as if Mom had been crying.

Dad said, "Ricky, Koko was a very sick dog and was in great pain. I'm so sorry to tell you that Koko died today. He passed away peacefully in my arms."

Tears streamed down Rick's face. He wanted to say something, but the lump in his throat wouldn't let him. He picked up Koko's squeaky bone, ran upstairs and threw himself onto the bed. That night, he sobbed himself to sleep, with Koko's squeaky bone tucked firmly under his pillow.

Over the next few days, the house felt strange. Nobody barked when the mailman walked past. No clicky-clack of claws on the kitchen floor. No wet nose at the table every time food was served. Mom and Dad did their best to cheer up Rick. Besides, Christmas was just days away! But it was no good. He missed Koko terribly.

The night before Christmas, Rick shuffled past the brightly lit tree, barely noticing the twinkling lights. This was going to be the worst Christmas, ever!

Later that night, Rick woke suddenly. He thought he heard the squeaky bone! From under the bed came a snuffling sound. Rick leaned over and came face to face with a scruffy old yellow Lab – with Koko's squeaky bone in his mouth!

"Hrmmphy," said the dog. He dropped the squeaky toy out of his mouth and tried again. "Howdy."

"Howdy?" said Rick, confused. "I've never heard a dog speak before."

"All dogs speak, you just don't listen properly," replied the dog.

A foul stench filled the room. Rick choked and covered his nose with a corner of the bed spread. He looked at the big dog suspiciously. "Was that you?"

"All dogs fart, too."

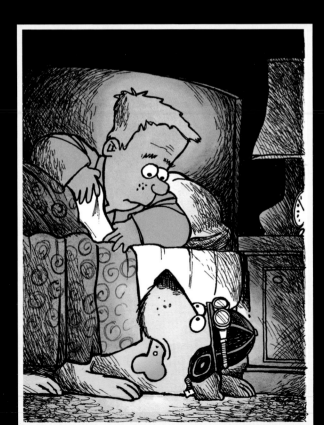

The strange dog picked up the squeaky toy and wandered toward the open window. Rick jumped to his feet and snatched the bone out of the dog's mouth.

"That's Koko's toy. Not yours! Ugh. You drool almost as badly as Koko." He wiped the bone off on his pajamas.

The dog smiled. "I know, I'm taking him his squeaky bone. He forgot it."

"But, but Koko is…"

"At the Rainbow Bridge."

Rick stared at the big dog. "No, Koko is dead!" He paused. "What's the Rainbow Bridge?"

"Not for you to know. Now give me back that bone, I must be going."

Rick put his arms around the old dog's neck. "Please, take me with you!"

"Sorry, that's against the rules." The dog leaned back, poised to leap out the window. Rick jumped on his back and clung on for dear life as the dog cleared the window. Rick braced himself to hit the ground, but to his amazement the dog hovered in mid-air. Rick hung on to the dog's smelly fur tightly. The dog turned to Rick. "Okay, if you insist, but you have to promise you won't tell anyone what you're about to see."

"Yes, I promise." Rick peered down at the yard far below him. "Are you sure this is safe?"

"Been doing dog-toy pick-ups for years. Hold on tight!"

The dog loped through the air. The town slept below them, with only a few outside dogs barking greetings as they passed overhead. Faster and higher they flew, climbing through the clouds. The air got chilly and Rick buried his face in the dog's neck, immediately emerging to spit out a wad of fur.

"Pfft! You need a brushing, big-time."

The dog turned around and shrugged.

"Nobody has to get brushed at the Rainbow Bridge."

Rick wasn't sure how they got from
clouds to soft grass, but suddenly he was
looking down on a bright green meadow.

The dog came in for a landing, hitting the ground hard,
sending them both tumbling on the soft grass. Rick
picked himself up, brushed daisies out of his hair and
looked around in amazement.

The meadow was filled with sounds of barking, twittering and meowing. It was alive with birds, dogs, cats, mice, gerbils, in fact, almost every kind of critter you could imagine having as a pet.

Suddenly, from among the ruckus, Rick heard a very familiar bark.

15

From out of the crowd of critters, a dog bounded toward him.

Rick opened his arms wide. "Koko!"

Koko leaped on Rick, knocking him to the ground, and proceeded to give him a good face-licking. Then Koko sat up, looked at Rick and cocked his head.

"I thought Buster was just bringing back my squeaky bone – but he brought you back too!" Koko lowered his voice. "You're not supposed to be here, Ricky."

Rick looked around him. "Where is here, Koko?"

"The Rainbow Bridge."

Rick looked puzzled. "What's the Rainbow Bridge?"

"It's not a what, it's a place. Come on, I'll show you."

Koko trotted off down a path, and Rick followed. They climbed over a rise in the meadow to see an enormous mountain of bones. It must have been as high as a house! Lying around the bone pile, dogs of all sizes were chewing happily.

Koko licked his lips. "You never run out of bones at the Rainbow Bridge."

They continued down the path. A whizzing noise filled the air and a pair of dogs raced past them, chasing a Frisbee. More whizzing and more Frisbees flew by, followed by more dogs. Rick looked up the hill. At the top was a large mechanical Frisbee-throwing device, operated by a dog pedalling a pulley device.

"The machine never gets tired of throwing them. Unlike some people I know." Koko looked sideways at Rick, who pretended not to hear.

Rick stepped off the path to get a better view and jumped as a cat paw appeared out of the foliage and swiped his ankle.

"Watch it, Ricky. You're stepping on catnip."

Rolling fields of catnip stretched as far as Rick could see, with cat tails contentedly waving above the catnip. Beyond it, rabbits were happily hopping about among the daisies.

Rick gingerly followed Koko over a log bridge into a lush forest, where thousands of birds fluttered about. Budgies, finches, parrots, all happily crowded the branches. The sound of their singing was almost deafening.

Rick stopped in front of a heap of couches.
The sides had been shredded by cat claws
and almost every couch was occupied by
snoozing dogs or cats. Koko pawed at a
cushion. "We call this our lounge area."

"And no one tells you to get off the couch?"

"At first, I felt a bit guilty," said Koko, "but it
soon passes."

Koko stopped by a clear running stream and plunged his head into it. Bubbles came up from under the water. Koko lifted his head. "You'll love this, Ricky."

Rick shook his head. "Thanks, but I'm not thirsty."

"No, remember that goldfish you had when you were three?"

"Bob? Yes, Bob was the best goldfish, ever. I really miss Bob."

"Well, stick your head in the water and say hello to Bob!"

Rick took a deep breath and stuck his head in the water. Sure enough, Bob swam up to him, wiggled his tail and blew a stream of bubbles at Rick, which tickled his nose.

Rick didn't know what to say. "Everyone looks so happy. But what are you all doing here?"

Koko casually lifted his leg to pee on one of the many brightly painted fire hydrants that lined the path through the meadow. "Waiting for those who loved us to turn up."

Rick was about to say something, when a bell tolled in the distance.

The meadow came alive with animals and Rick was almost bowled over by the crowd that was loping, scampering and scuttling across the meadow, all heading in the same direction.

Koko pulled Rick's sleeve. "C'mon, Rick, it's pick-up time!"

From out of the mist that marked the end of the meadow, a very old lady appeared, looking about nervously, unsure of where she was.

Suddenly an old cat raced out of the catnip meadow toward the old lady, but at the last minute remembered she was a cat and slowed to a casual stroll. She couldn't contain her excitement, though, and she leapt into the old lady's arms.

"Muffin!" The old lady was thrilled to see her cat again.

Koko chuckled. "I'm going to miss Muffin. She played the best game of tag."

An old man seemed to appear out of nowhere. Koko sighed. "Finally."

A small, scruffy dog raced toward the old man, who exclaimed, "Scout! You're here!"

Koko beamed. "Scout has been waiting here the longest."

Rick looked at the old lady and old man, now happily playing with their long-lost pets. "But, Koko, who are these people?"

Koko wagged his tail. "Just as a faithful pet gets old and passes on, so too must their human companions."

After much purring and licking, the old man and his dog, and old lady and her cat stepped off the meadow and onto a bridge that stretched past a rainbow and into the shimmering haze in the distance. All the dogs barked goodbye and wagged their tails furiously. The cats, of course, pretended not to notice, but if you listened carefully, you could hear them contentedly purring.

"Where are they going, Koko?"

"They're going to a happy place, where they will always be together."

"Can we go too?" asked Rick.

Koko shook his head firmly. "No. It's not your time, Ricky. Go home and live a long and wonderful life. I'll always be waiting for you here at the Rainbow Bridge. But now you must go, there is someone very special waiting for you."

In silence, Rick and Koko watched the old couple and their pets until they disappeared in the haze.

A loud fart announced that Buster had returned.

"Climb on, Rick. I'm taking you home," said Buster.

Koko licked Rick's hand one more time and looked up into Rick's eyes.

"And Ricky, have lots of pets and love them all like you loved me."

Buster rose into the air, the scene below began to fade and the barks and chirps seemed to echo in the distance.

But before it faded completely, Rick heard one last happy bark from Koko.

Rick woke up in his own bed and looked around him. He felt under his pillow for the squeaky bone. It wasn't there! He looked down at his pajamas and gingerly picked off a large clump of smelly, yellow dog fur. It wasn't a dream!

The sound of Christmas music drifted up from the stereo downstairs.

"It's Christmas morning!"

Rick raced downstairs, bursting to tell his parents everything that happened last night. But he paused at the Christmas tree. He had promised Buster he wouldn't tell anyone what he had seen.

Mom and Dad were in the kitchen and sitting in front of them was a shaggy dog with a goofy grin on his face. The dog looked up at Rick and wagged his tail. Dad looked down at the dog.

"We saw him at the animal shelter, Ricky. He was all alone and needs a good home. Would you like to take care of him?"

Rick grinned from ear to ear. "He's beautiful. I'm going to call him…"

A terrible smell filled the room and the dog wagged his tail contentedly. Rick wrinkled his nose. "I'm going to call him… Buster! Buster, want to go for a walk?"

Buster jumped up and down and yipped happily.

Dad looked at Mom. "You'd almost think Buster understands what Ricky is saying."

Rick looked at his parents. "All dogs speak, we just don't listen properly. Come on, Buster!"

The two raced outside to throw snowballs and build snowmen.

It was the perfect winter for a boy and his dog.